For Jonah

All rights reserved. Published in the United States by Random House Studio, an imprint of
Random House Children's Books, a division of Penguin Random House LLC, New York.

Random House Studio with colophon is a registered trademark of Penguin Random House LLC.

GRUMPY MONKEY is a registered trademark of Pick & Flick Pictures, Inc.

Visit us on the Web! rhcbooks.com

Educators and librarians, for a variety of teaching tools, visit us at RHTeachersLibrarians.com

Library of Congress Cataloging-in-Publication Data is available upon request.
ISBN 978-0-593-70928-3 (trade) — ISBN 978-0-593-70929-0 (lib. bdg.) —
ISBN 978-0-593-70930-6 (ebook)

The text of this book is set in 18-point Bernhard Gothic.
Book design by Nicole Gastonguay

MANUFACTURED IN CHINA

10 9 8 7 6 5 4 3 2 1
First Edition

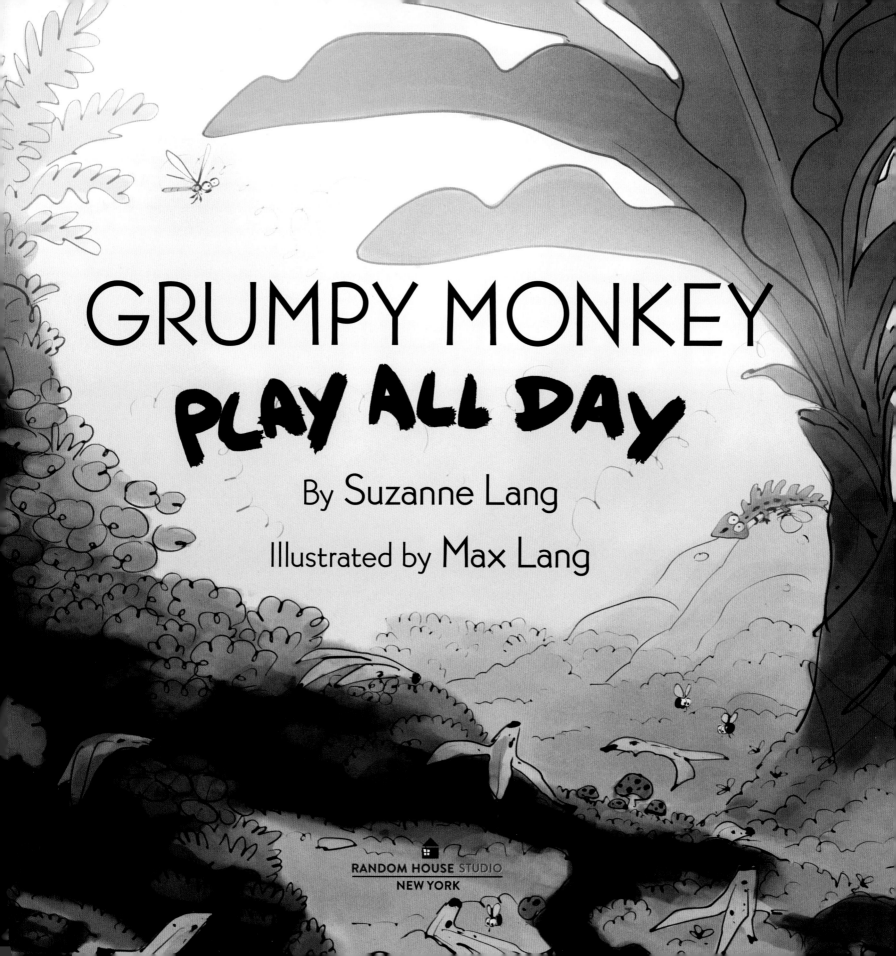

GRUMPY MONKEY
PLAY ALL DAY

By Suzanne Lang

Illustrated by Max Lang

RANDOM HOUSE STUDIO
NEW YORK

It was a busy afternoon in the jungle. Jim Panzee had to tidy his branch, search for food, clean his teeth, and pick fleas out of his fur. Jim didn't want to do any of that.

"I kind of like cleaning my branch," said Norman from next door.

"I don't," said Jim. "It's boring. Plus every time I clean it, it just gets messy again."

And there was lots of fun to be had.

"You should sing with us!"
said the birds.

Jim had fun singing.

"You should swing with us!" said the monkeys.

Jim had fun swinging.

"You should roll with us!" said the zebras.

Jim had fun rolling.

"You should stroll with us!"
said the peacocks.

Jim had fun strolling.

"Having fun is the best!" shouted Jim.

But then the others had to stop.

"We have to clean our nests," said the birds.

"We need to graze," said the zebras.

"It's time for our nap," said the monkeys.

"We're an absolute mess. We must go and preen," said the peacocks.

"Be boring if you want to," said Jim.

"I'm going to play with someone else."

And there were plenty of animals
to play with.

"You should kick sand!"

"You should
catch leaves!"

"You should stomp your feet!"

"You should jump up
and down!"

"You should play tag!"

Jim played and played.
He was having a great time . . .

. . . but then his tummy rumbled.

"Maybe we should find some food,"
suggested Marabou.

"No!" said Jim. "Finding food is boring.
I'm having fun!"

Jim tried to play ball, but he
was so itchy he kept dropping it.

"Fleas," said Warthog. "Maybe pick them?"
"No, that's boring!" said Jim. "I'm having fun!"

Jim jumped up and down, but then he
stopped suddenly.
  "Bathroom break?" Bullfrog suggested.
  "I don't need a bathroom break!"
said Jim. "I'm having fun!"

"You don't look like you're having much fun, Jim," said the other animals.

I AM HAVING FUN!

Jim shouted.

And then he fell to the ground.
Jim was exhausted. He was hungry.
His throat hurt. He was itchy and dirty
and cold.

"Playing all day isn't really all that fun," Jim sighed.

"Too much of anything can be, well, too much," said Norman.

And so Jim did all the
things he needed to do.

He took a bathroom break.

He found bananas to eat and even picked his teeth after.

He took a bath and plucked the fleas out of his fur.

And finally he tidied his branch
so he could go to sleep.
None of it was fun.

But Jim felt great afterward.